Kintu
and the
Fairy Bee

- -

MARY BETH NUMBERS   *Illustrated by Kabuye Ivan*

Dedication

For survivors everywhere who often rely on the advice of a friend, but most especially for my daughter, Christa Numbers Preston, who models the strength achieved by embracing other cultures and accepting every individual for their talents and abilities. M B N

For my wife, Nalubega Shakirah, and my son, Ssebunya Aaron. K I

Acknowledgements

This book evolved from my attempts as an elementary teacher from the United States to meaningfully connect with students with disabilities in Uganda. We enjoyed a shared synergy through the annual retelling of the simple stories of their folklore, enhanced with communication board visuals. As I told the story in English, the talented teachers of the St. Ursula School translated it into Lugandan to enhance the students' understanding. I value those first cultural exchanges with Sister Lucy and teachers Milton, Joshua, Sylivia, Esther, Monica and Andrew.

I am indebted to Mrs. George Baskerville, who first published this story in 1922. She credits the writing of Sir Apolo Kagwa, K.C.M.G., M.B.E., Katikiro of Buganda and the rich oral storytelling traditions of many generations.

I also acknowledge the contribution of illustrator, Kabuye Ivan. I first learned of his talents through his acrylic canvases sold on the streets of Jinja, Uganda. Later he volunteered to beautify the Home of Hope orphanage in Jinja. Under his direction a handful of volunteers painted a mural entrance to this haven. This is a welcoming place where children with special needs are nurtured. Kabuye continues to inspire many with his willingness to share his talents for the benefit of individuals with disabilities throughout Uganda.

Kintu
and the
Fairy Bee

Many years ago, when the land around the Great Lake was uninhabited, a strong young man named Kintu roamed near its shores and decided it was a fine place to make his home. Kintu was quite alone. He had only one cow that was a fine companion.

One day, while planting crops in the fields, Kintu became friends with a bumblebee. There had been a great rainstorm, and the drops knocked the poor bee to the ground on his back. Try as he might, the bee could not get up again. He lay in a puddle and would have died of the wet and cold. Feeling sorry for the bee, Kintu picked him up and held him in his warm hands. Soon the bumblebee felt better and said to Kintu, "You have saved my life. I will be your friend. From this day on, I will help you when you are in trouble."

One morning Kintu woke up and his cow was gone. He could not find it anywhere. It was then that the bumblebee came to him and said, "I will help you find your cow. It has been stolen by the witch who lives on the Mountain of the Moon, where the snow never melts."

So Kintu took his stick and set out on his long journey to the far-away mountains near the Congo. The bumblebee flew before him to show him the way.

On they went, day after day, through dark forests and over wide rivers, and by narrow paths through the jungle grass, until they saw the Mountains of the Moon in the far distance.

Then the bumblebee said to Kintu, "Do everything that I tell you, for you must outsmart the witch. If you are not smarter than him, he will never give you back your cow."

When they arrived in the witch's country, the great mountains were towering above them. Kintu saw that it was a rich country with great herds of cattle and flocks of sheep and goats, and beautiful gardens, and many people.

When the witch heard that Kintu had arrived, he sent for him and said, "Are you really Kintu, the man who lives all alone with only one cow?"

Kintu said, "Yes, I am, and you have stolen my cow, and I have come to find it."

The witch paused and thought. "This is a wonderful man. We will see how clever he is. How did he find his way to my mountains from the Great Lake? How did he know that I stole his cow while he was asleep, for there was no one to tell him? I will test him and see if he really is a wise man."

So the witch gave Kintu a house in which to rest and said, "I will bring you some supper."

Kintu rested a little while, and then to his surprise, one thousand people arrived, each carrying a basket of cooked food.

"The witch has sent you your supper," they said, and put down the one thousand baskets.

"Thank them very much," whispered the bee in Kintu's ear, "and tell them to come back in a little while to fetch their baskets."

So the people went away wondering, "How is it possible for one man to eat so much?"

Kintu was upset, for he had no idea how to consume all this food, but the bee had a plan. The fairy bee called on all the ants in the country.

First, he called the red ants that live in the forests and are always hungry, for they can eat a dead elephant if they find it.

Next, he called the white ants that build big castles for themselves of red earth which look like huts on the hillsides. In the middle of these castles is a beautiful room with smooth walls where their Queen lives.

Then he called the large black ants that run very fast and lose their
way every two minutes and run back again to find it.

Finally, he called the little black ants that are always watching and run out quickly to pick
up a crumb or a seed or a grain of corn each time they see these on the ground.

All these ants came in hordes and they carried away the food until the
baskets were all empty except one, which Kintu ate for his supper.

Then the witch came back and shouted when he saw the empty baskets piled up together, "How can one man eat so much? This man must also be a witch."

So the old witch reacted, as any good host must, and agreed. "You are a marvelous man, I will not tease you any more. If you can recognize your cow in my herd, you may take it back and go home to your fields."

The witch rounded up all the cows, and Kintu was told to go find his cow. The bumblebee flew before Kintu as he made his way amongst the herd. There were many, many cows, with long horns all standing upright and huddled together tightly.

Then the bumblebee stopped on the horn of one of the cows. Kintu saw the signal of his old friend and said to the witch, "This is my cow that you stole from me while I slept."

The witch was astonished that he could find just the right one. The witch had to be true to his word, so he gave Kintu his cow and bid them goodbye. The bumblebee was able to lead Kintu home.

So it is said that even today if you journey to the Mountains of the Moon and climb to the bamboo forests, the trees will lean down to touch you and whisper to each other, "This is Kintu, this is Kintu, this is Kintu!" Forever, they remember the first man who outwitted the witch and they hope he has returned to keep them safe again.